LOVE IS MY FAVOURITE THING

Emma Chichester Clark

JONATHAN CAPE
LONDON

For my two grandpas,
age 602 and 637
in dog years.

Emma Chichester Clark began the website **Plumdog Blog** in 2012, chronicling the real-life
adventures of her lovable "whoosell", (whippet, Jack Russell and poodle cross) Plum.
Emma soon gained thousands of loyal Plumdog devotees, and in 2014 a book of the blog was
published by Jonathan Cape. This picture book story is the first Plumdog book for children.

JONATHAN CAPE

UK | USA | Canada | Ireland | Australia
India | New Zealand | South Africa
Jonathan Cape is part of the Penguin Random House group of companies
whose addresses can be found at global.penguinrandomhouse.com.
www.penguin.co.uk   www.puffin.co.uk   www.ladybird.co.uk

Penguin
Random House
UK

First published 2015
Paperback edition published 2016
This mini hardback edition published 2017
001

Printed in China
A CIP catalogue record for this book is available from the British Library

ISBN: 978-0-857-55193-1

All correspondence to:
Jonathan Cape, Penguin Random House Children's
80 Strand, London WC2R 0RL

MIX
Paper from
responsible sources
FSC® C018179

I AM PLUM,
but I love being called Plummie.

And **LOVE** is my favourite thing.

I love all kinds
of weather,
especially wind.

But I don't
really like rain.

I love snow,

and I love sun.

I love my bear,   and my bed.

I love treats,   and
                            catching,

I love sticks
SO much,

BUT LOVE IS MY VERY FAVOURITE THING!

I love Sam and Gracie, who live next door.

I love it when they come through the hedge
to play at my house.

And I love Emma and Rupert.
They are my mummy and daddy.
I love it when they say,
"You are a very good girl, Plummie!"
Then, I feel loved all over,
and **LOVE** is my favourite thing.

I love the park and my friends.
I love the grass and the trees.
I love it when Emma says, "Good girl, Plummie!"
when I do a poo, as if it's so, so clever.

I know it means she loves me
and **LOVE** is my favourite thing.

But yesterday, **EVERYTHING** went wrong.

When Emma said, "Don't go in the pond, Plummie!" I wasn't listening.

No, Plum!

I heard Rocket say, "Come on, Plum! Come on! Come on!"

Come back, Plum!

And I just couldn't help it. I really couldn't.

Water is one of my other favourite things! I love it! I LOVE it!

"Isn't this great?" said Rocket. And it was. It really was...

...until Emma arrived. "BAD GIRL!" she shouted, and I knew I'd made a BIG mistake.

She marched me home.
The whole world was **black**.
Will she still love me?

Sam and Gracie
heard what I'd done.
"Oh, Plum!" said Gracie.
"Oh, Plum!" said Sam.
Will they still love me?

I ran to find them
a present but...

...there was only a cushion.
When Gracie tried
to take it...

...I just couldn't help it!
I really couldn't. It's one
of my favourite games!

I love it! I LOVE it!
"No! Plum!" cried Gracie.

"No! No, PLUM!" cried Sam.
They were pulling and I was
pulling...

...Sam was shouting and I was flying
and SUDDENLY...

"PLUM!" shouted Emma.

"VERY BAD GIRL!" she said.

"OUT YOU GO!"
said Emma,
and I realised I'd made
a dreadful mistake.
"Oh, Plum!" said Gracie.
"Oh, Plum!" said Sam.

Will any of them
still love me?

It seemed like forever but finally we all went to the park. It was sunny and bright and everywhere I looked I saw tiddlers with ice-creams. "Plummie," said Emma. "That's not for you!"

But I really
love ice-cream.
I know all
about it.

I know what
it tastes like
and I love it!

I just
LOVE it!

And tiddlers are **always** dropping things...

...they drop things **right** in front of me...

...and I just couldn't help it. I really couldn't ...so I grabbed it!

"PLUM!" cried Emma.
Then everyone was running
and everyone was chasing!

I ran to my house
and waited and waited.
I knew that I'd made

**THE MOST ABSOLUTELY
AWFUL MISTAKE!**

"Oh, Plum!" said Gracie.

"Oh, Plum!"
said Sam.

"Oh, Plum!"
said Emma.

"What will your daddy say?"
said Emma. "What a **BAD** girl!"
The children just
looked at me.

They'd all had
enough of me.

They marched me downstairs
and sent me to bed.

Eventually,
they came
and opened
the door.

"Well, Plum,"
said my daddy.
"Are you sorry?"
he asked.

And I was. I really was.
I'd do **ANYTHING!**
as long as they
still love me.

"BUT DO YOU STILL
LOVE ME?

DO YOU STILL
LOVE ME?

DO YOU STILL
LOVE ME?"

"Oh, Plummie!" said Emma.
"Oh, Plummie!" said my daddy.
"We do love you!
But – you've got to get better
and do as you're told, and

BE A GOOD GIRL!"

So I do try to be good.
I don't always remember – I wish that I could.
I still make mistakes and I still love ice-cream
and swimming, but I know they love me.
They do! They really do!

AND THAT'S WHY LOVE IS MY
VERY, VERY, VERY FAVOURITE THING!